STAR WARS®

THE CLONE WARS™

HERO OF THE CONFEDERACY
VOLUME TWO

A HERO RISES

SCRIPT
HENRY GILROY
STEVEN MELCHING

PENCILS
BRIAN KOSCHAK

INKS
DAN PARSONS

COLORS
MICHAEL E. WIGGAM

LETTERING
MICHAEL HEISLER

COVER ART
RUSSELL CHONG

A new crisis! Chancellor Palpatine's order to blockade neutral worlds that trade with the Separatists has driven dozens of wealthy systems toward an alliance with Count Dooku. Among those worlds is Valahari, whose ruler, Viscount Harko Vane, and his family are old friends of Obi-Wan Kenobi.

Forced to blockade Valahari, Obi-Wan and Anakin Skywalker were soon challenged by the Viscount. When Vane's ship suddenly exploded, Anakin was blamed and reassigned to a distant planet. The death of his father has driven Prince Tofen Vane—a pilot every bit as skillful as Anakin—to launch devastating attacks against the Republic.

As Tofen becomes a hero of the Confederacy, Obi-Wan seeks to uncover the truth about the mysterious explosion that claimed Harko Vane's life . . .

Spotlight

DARK HORSE COMICS

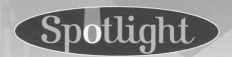

Visit us at www.abdopublishing.com

Reinforced library bound edition published in 2011 by Spotlight, a division of the ABDO Group, 8000 West 78th Street, Edina, Minnesota 55439. Spotlight produces high-quality reinforced library bound editions for schools and libraries. Published by agreement with Dark Horse Comics, Inc., and Lucasfilm Ltd.

Printed in the United States of America, North Mankato, Minnesota.
102010
012011
♻This book contains at least 10% recycled materials.

Cataloging-in-Publication Data

Gilroy, Henry.
 Hero of the Confederacy Vol. 2: a hero rises / story, Henry Gilroy and Steve Melching ; art, Brian Koschak. --Reinforced library bound ed.
   v. cm. -- (Star wars: the clone wars)
   "Dark Horse Comics."
 ISBN 978-1-59961-842-5 (v. 2)
 1. Graphic novels. [1. Graphic novels.] I. Melching, Steve. II. Koschak, Brian, ill. III. Star Wars, the clone wars (television program) IV. Title.
 PZ7.7.G55He 2011
 741.5'973

All Spotlight books have reinforced library bindings and are manufactured in the United States of America.

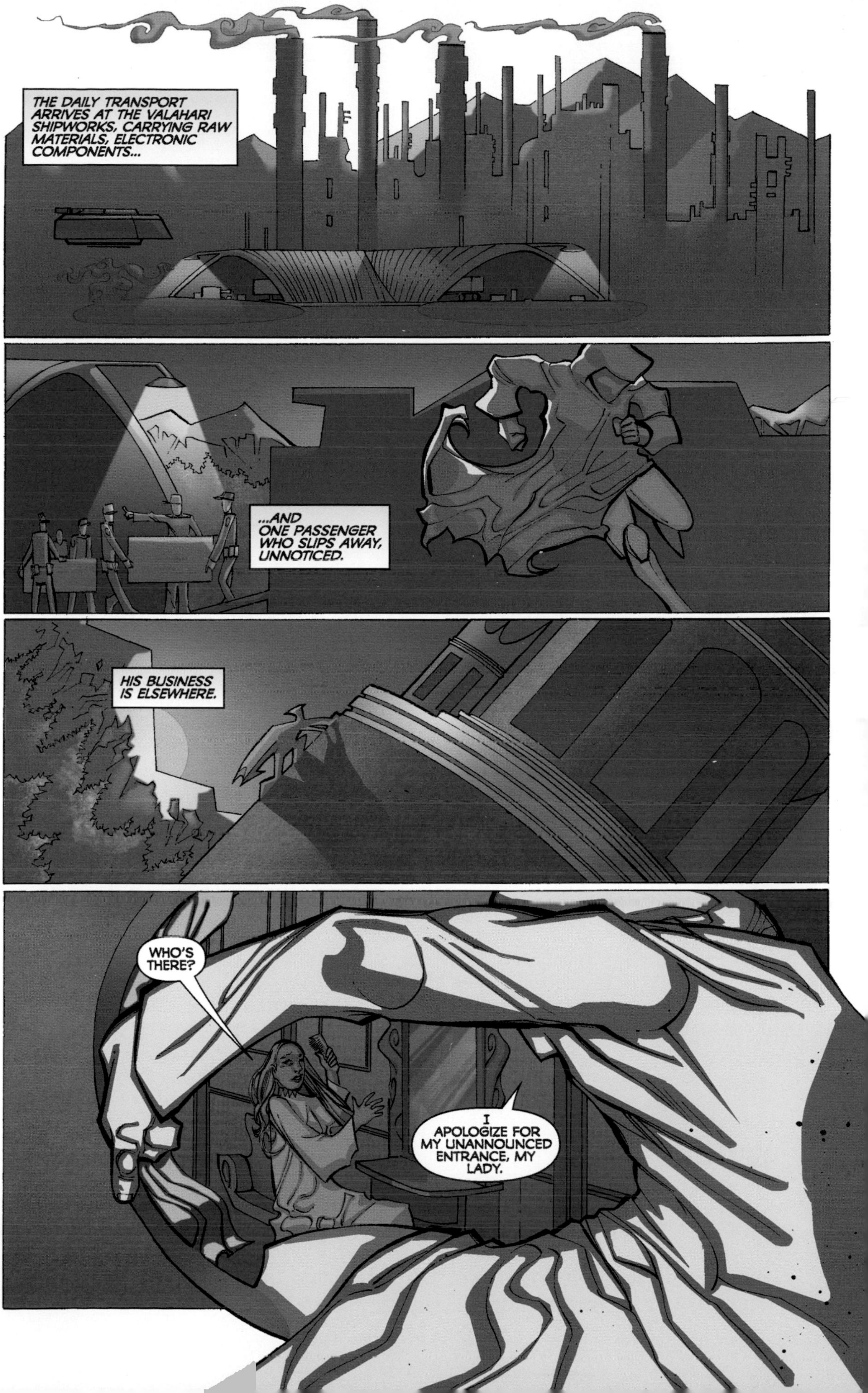
THE DAILY TRANSPORT ARRIVES AT THE VALAHARI SHIPWORKS, CARRYING RAW MATERIALS, ELECTRONIC COMPONENTS...
...AND ONE PASSENGER WHO SLIPS AWAY, UNNOTICED.
HIS BUSINESS IS ELSEWHERE.
WHO'S THERE?
I APOLOGIZE FOR MY UNANNOUNCED ENTRANCE, MY LADY.

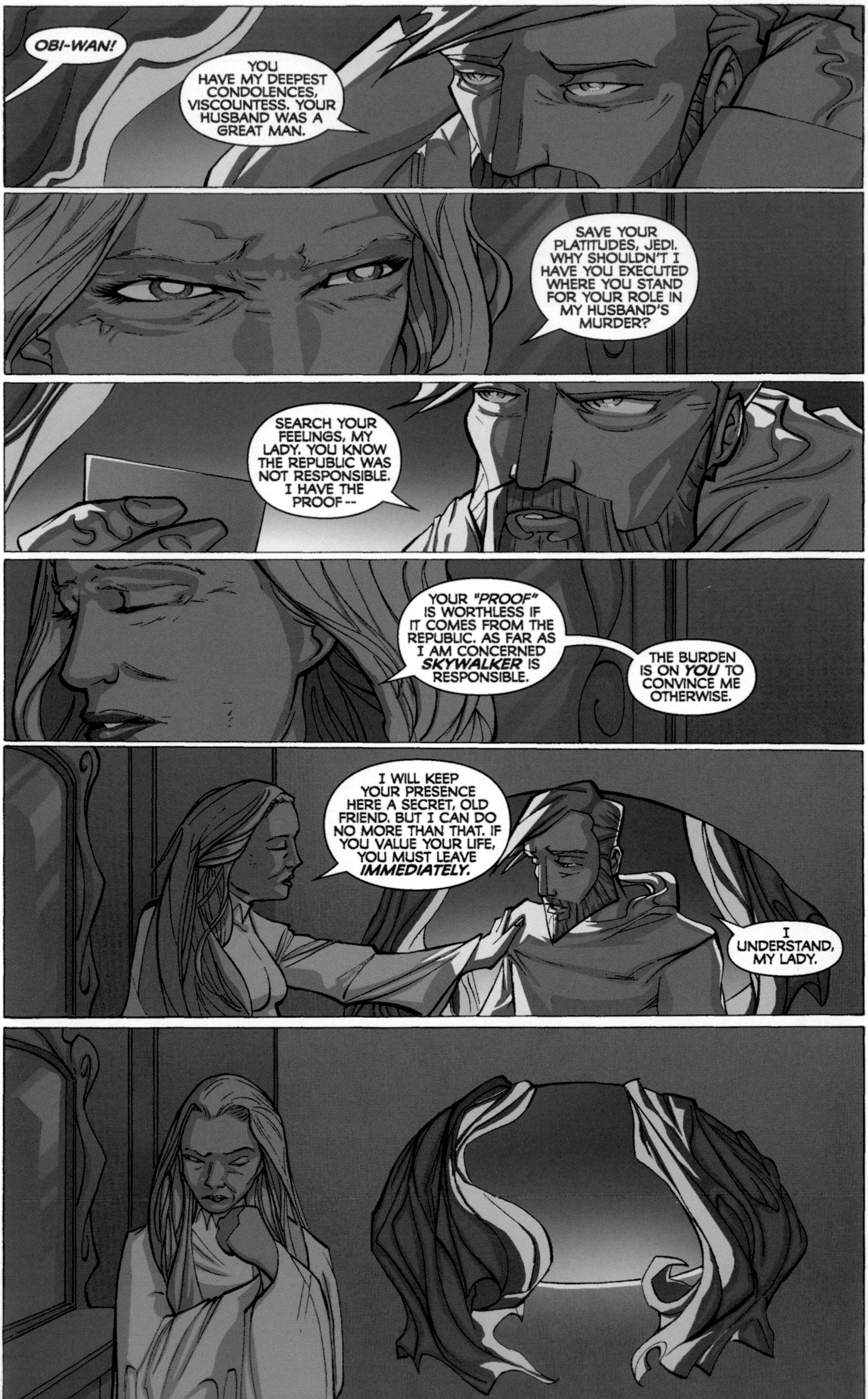
OBI-WAN!
YOU HAVE MY DEEPEST CONDOLENCES, VISCOUNTESS. YOUR HUSBAND WAS A GREAT MAN.
SAVE YOUR PLATITUDES, JEDI. WHY SHOULDN'T I HAVE YOU EXECUTED WHERE YOU STAND FOR YOUR ROLE IN MY HUSBAND'S MURDER?
SEARCH YOUR FEELINGS, MY LADY. YOU KNOW THE REPUBLIC WAS NOT RESPONSIBLE. I HAVE THE PROOF--
YOUR *"PROOF"* IS WORTHLESS IF IT COMES FROM THE REPUBLIC. AS FAR AS I AM CONCERNED *SKYWALKER* IS RESPONSIBLE.
THE BURDEN IS ON *YOU* TO CONVINCE ME OTHERWISE.
I WILL KEEP YOUR PRESENCE HERE A SECRET, OLD FRIEND. BUT I CAN DO NO MORE THAN THAT. IF YOU VALUE YOUR LIFE, YOU MUST LEAVE *IMMEDIATELY.*
I UNDERSTAND, MY LADY.

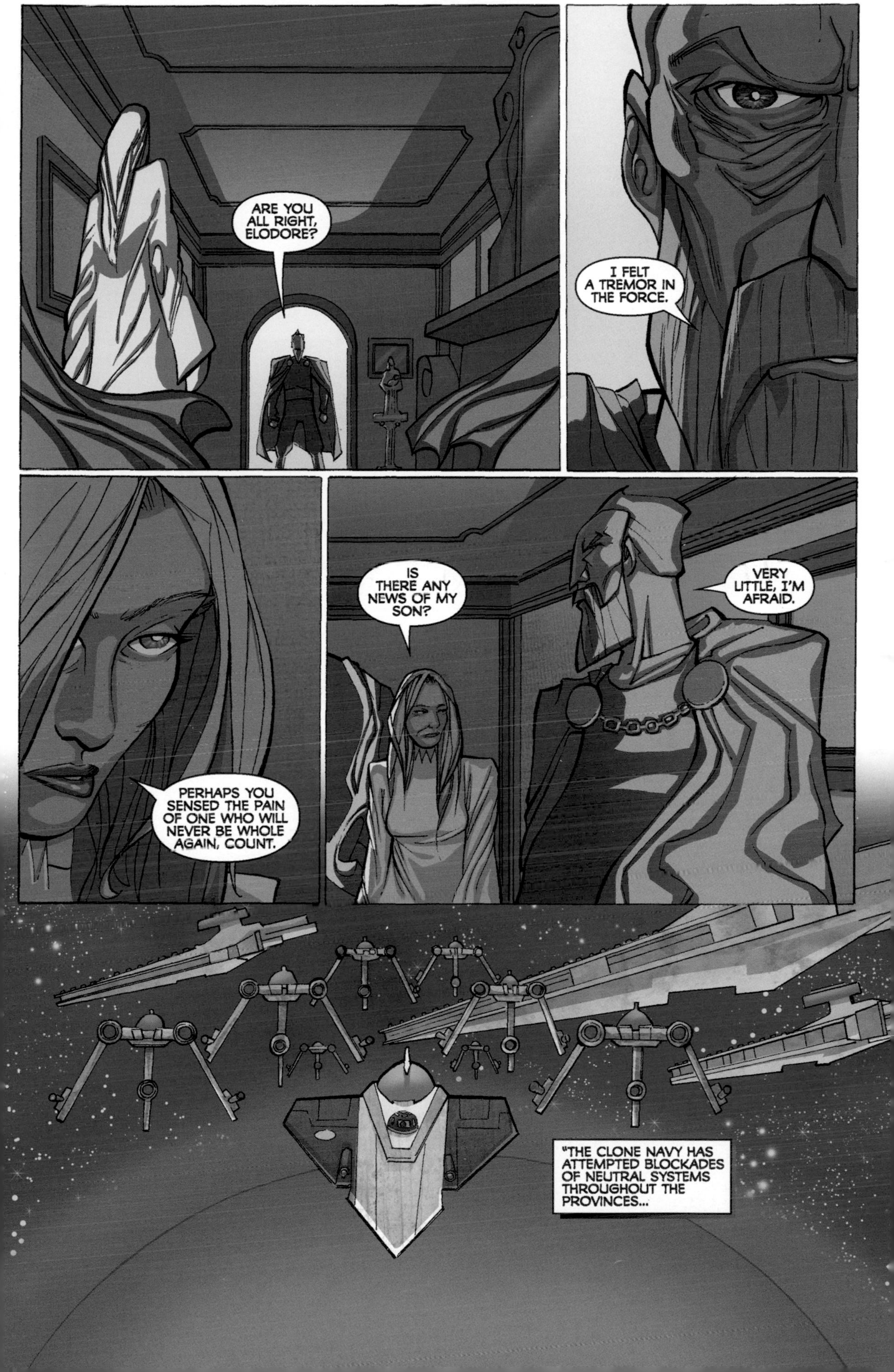
ARE YOU ALL RIGHT, ELODORE?
I FELT A TREMOR IN THE FORCE.
PERHAPS YOU SENSED THE PAIN OF ONE WHO WILL NEVER BE WHOLE AGAIN, COUNT.
IS THERE ANY NEWS OF MY SON?
VERY LITTLE, I'M AFRAID.
"THE CLONE NAVY HAS ATTEMPTED BLOCKADES OF NEUTRAL SYSTEMS THROUGHOUT THE PROVINCES...

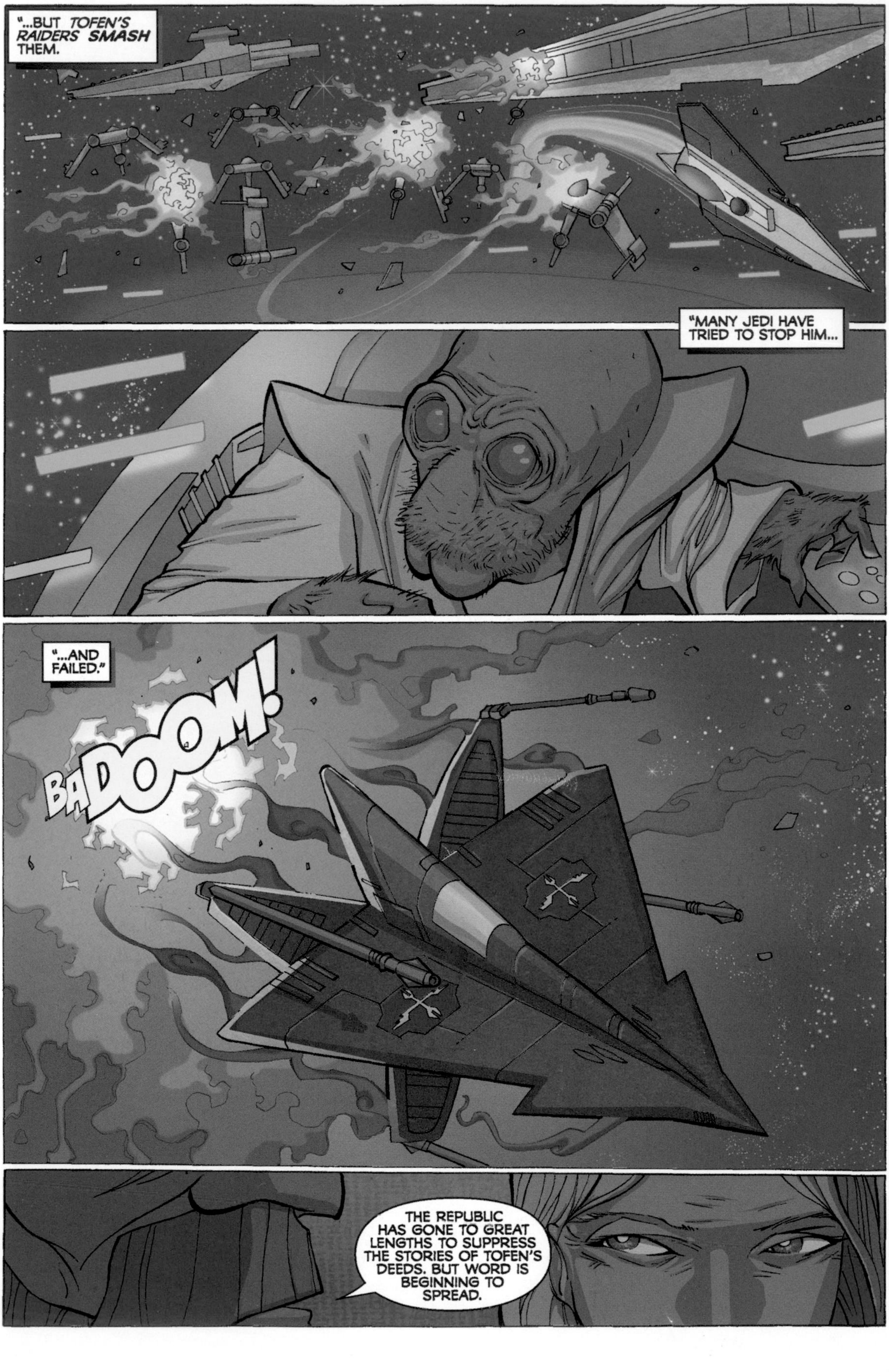
"...BUT TOFEN'S RAIDERS SMASH THEM.
"MANY JEDI HAVE TRIED TO STOP HIM...
"...AND FAILED."
BADOOM!
THE REPUBLIC HAS GONE TO GREAT LENGTHS TO SUPPRESS THE STORIES OF TOFEN'S DEEDS. BUT WORD IS BEGINNING TO SPREAD.

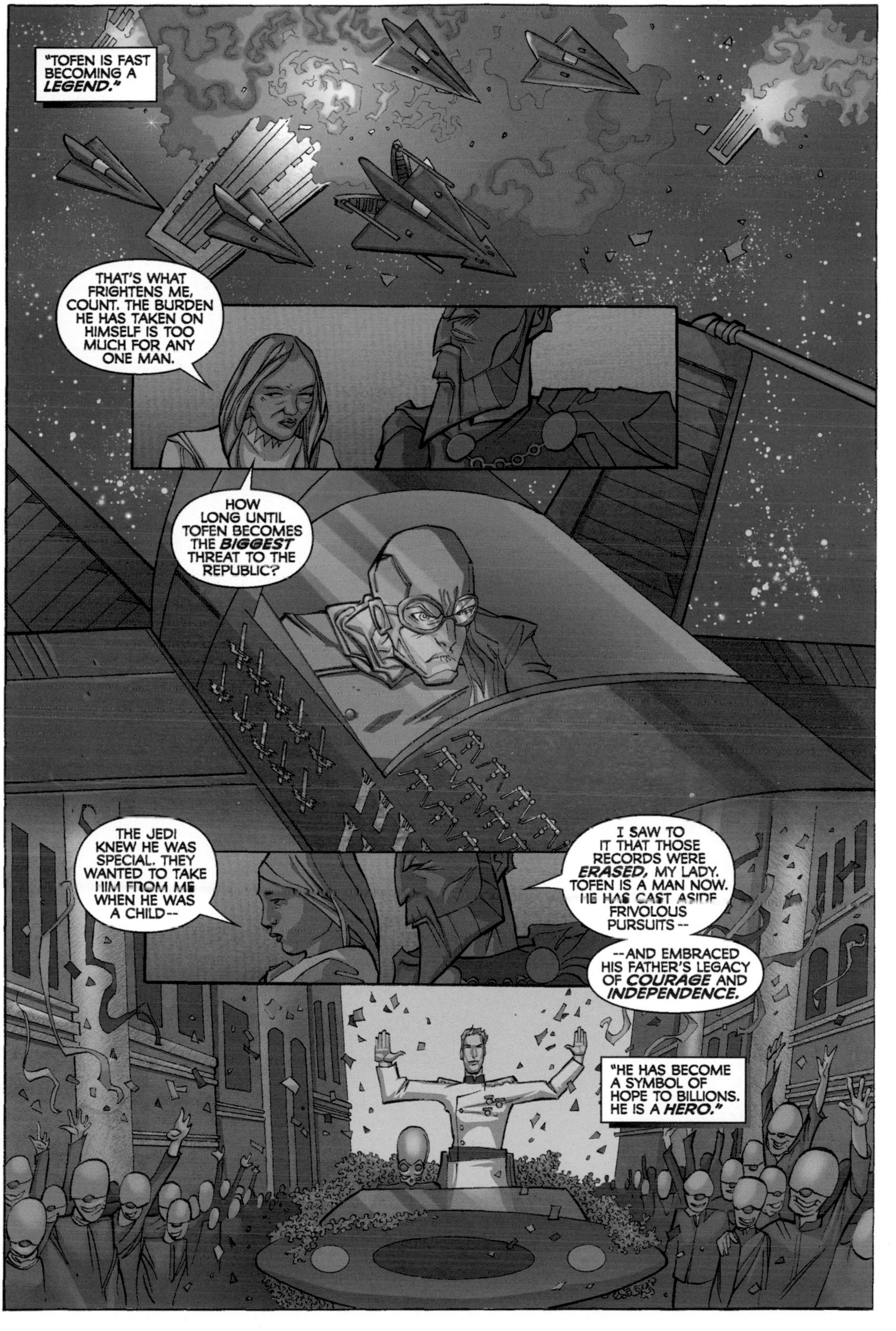
"TOFEN IS FAST BECOMING A *LEGEND.*"
THAT'S WHAT FRIGHTENS ME, COUNT. THE BURDEN HE HAS TAKEN ON HIMSELF IS TOO MUCH FOR ANY ONE MAN.
HOW LONG UNTIL TOFEN BECOMES THE *BIGGEST* THREAT TO THE REPUBLIC?
THE JEDI KNEW HE WAS SPECIAL. THEY WANTED TO TAKE HIM FROM ME WHEN HE WAS A CHILD--
I SAW TO IT THAT THOSE RECORDS WERE *ERASED,* MY LADY. TOFEN IS A MAN NOW. HE HAS CAST ASIDE FRIVOLOUS PURSUITS --
--AND EMBRACED HIS FATHER'S LEGACY OF *COURAGE* AND *INDEPENDENCE.*
"HE HAS BECOME A SYMBOL OF HOPE TO BILLIONS. HE IS A *HERO.*"

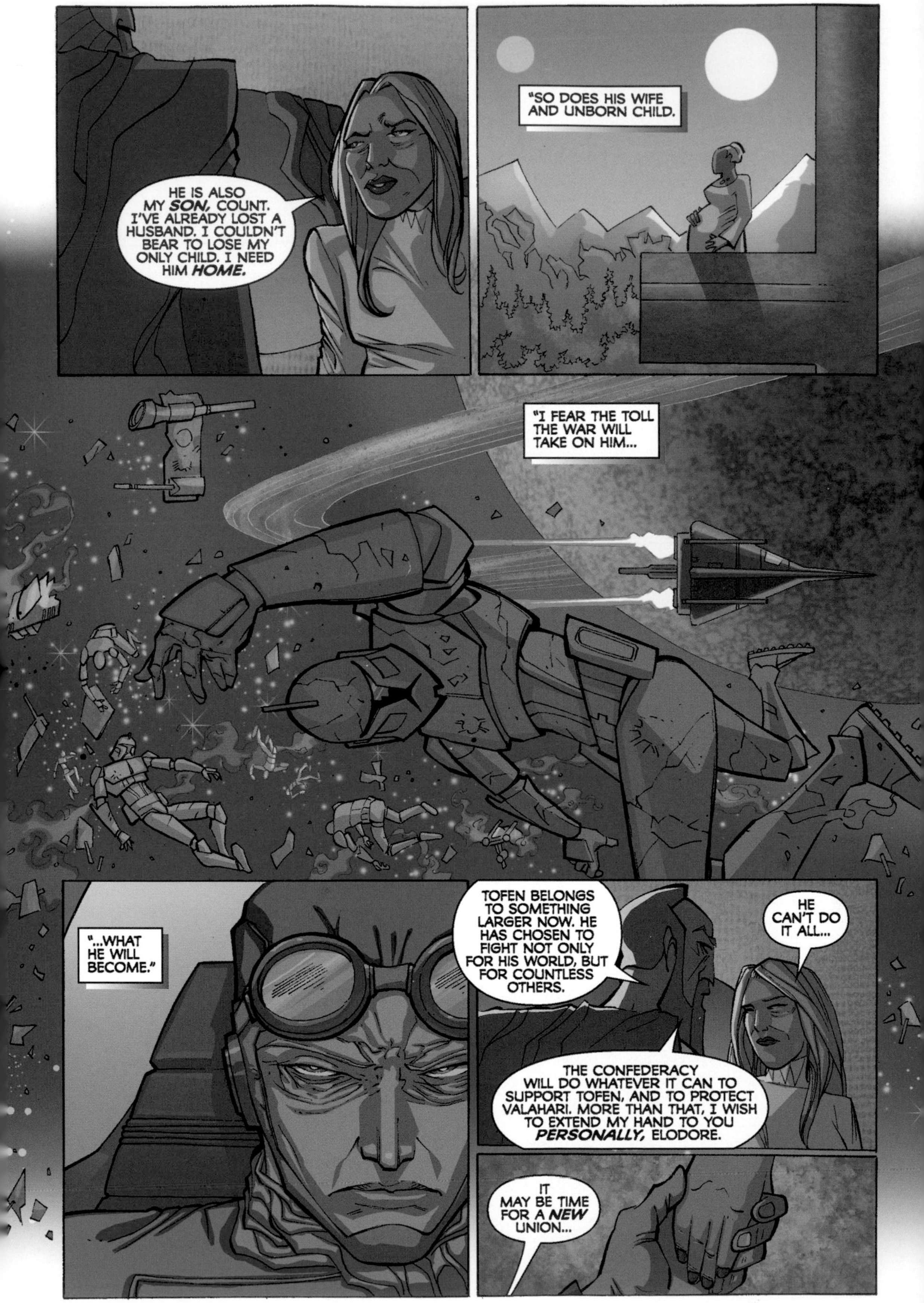
HE IS ALSO MY *SON,* COUNT. I'VE ALREADY LOST A HUSBAND. I COULDN'T BEAR TO LOSE MY ONLY CHILD. I NEED HIM *HOME.*
"SO DOES HIS WIFE AND UNBORN CHILD.
"I FEAR THE TOLL THE WAR WILL TAKE ON HIM...
"...WHAT HE WILL BECOME."
TOFEN BELONGS TO SOMETHING LARGER NOW. HE HAS CHOSEN TO FIGHT NOT ONLY FOR HIS WORLD, BUT FOR COUNTLESS OTHERS.
HE CAN'T DO IT ALL...
THE CONFEDERACY WILL DO WHATEVER IT CAN TO SUPPORT TOFEN, AND TO PROTECT VALAHARI. MORE THAN THAT, I WISH TO EXTEND MY HAND TO YOU *PERSONALLY,* ELODORE.
IT MAY BE TIME FOR A *NEW* UNION...

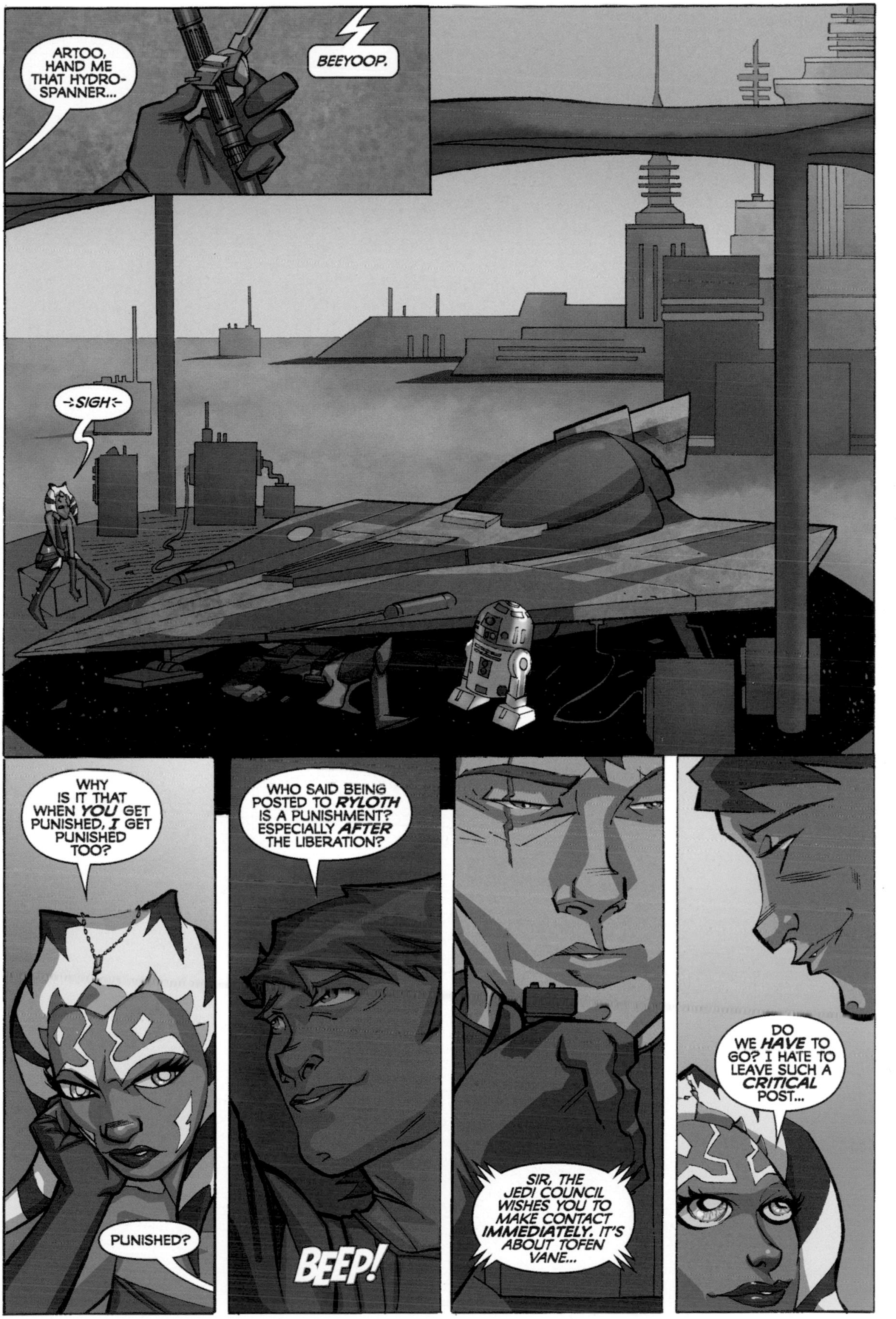
ARTOO, HAND ME THAT HYDRO-SPANNER...
BEEYOOP.
-SIGH-
WHY IS IT THAT WHEN YOU GET PUNISHED, I GET PUNISHED TOO?
PUNISHED?
WHO SAID BEING POSTED TO RYLOTH IS A PUNISHMENT? ESPECIALLY AFTER THE LIBERATION?
BEEP!
SIR, THE JEDI COUNCIL WISHES YOU TO MAKE CONTACT IMMEDIATELY. IT'S ABOUT TOFEN VANE...
DO WE HAVE TO GO? I HATE TO LEAVE SUCH A CRITICAL POST...

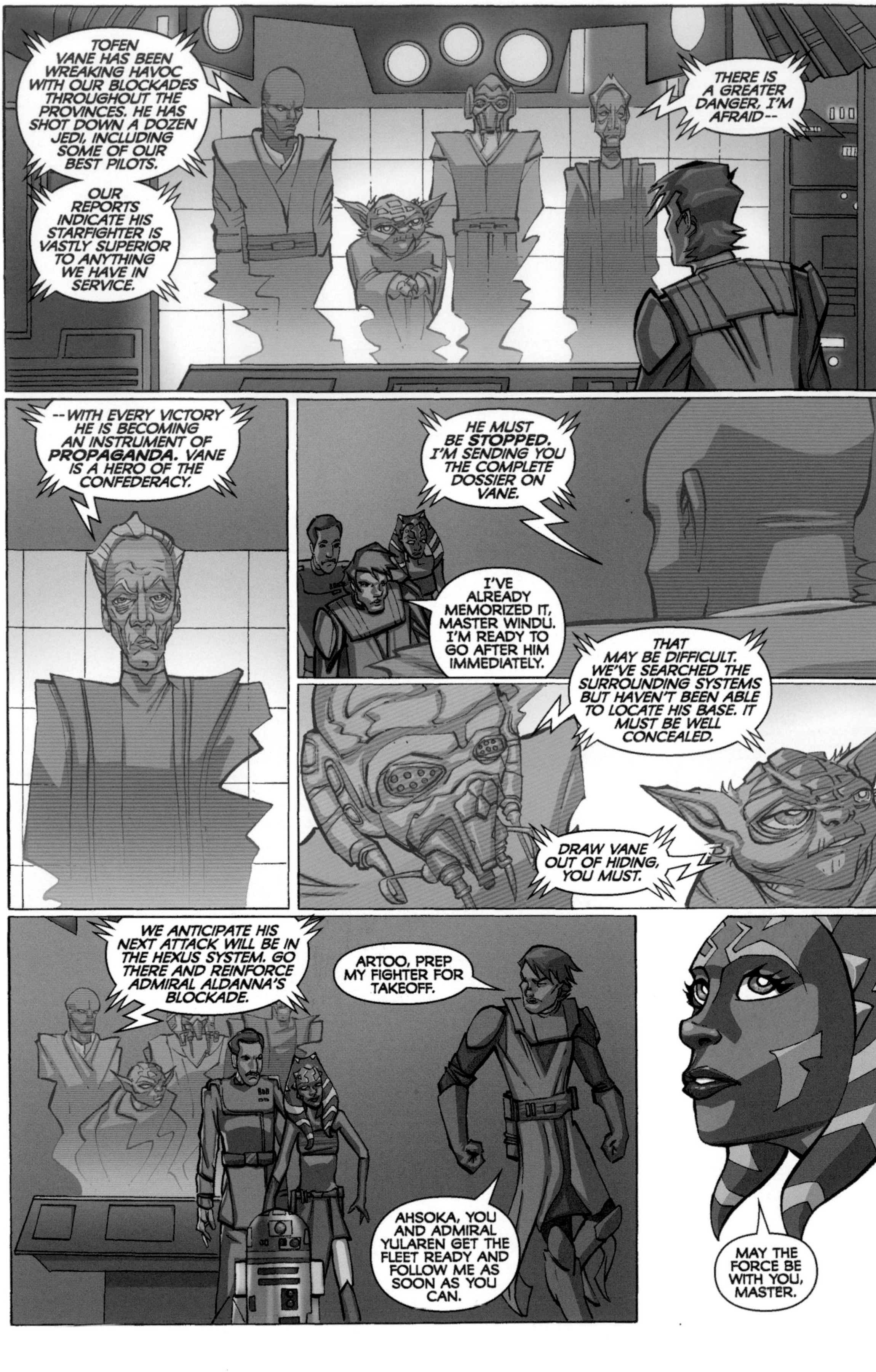
TOFEN VANE HAS BEEN WREAKING HAVOC WITH OUR BLOCKADES THROUGHOUT THE PROVINCES. HE HAS SHOT DOWN A DOZEN JEDI, INCLUDING SOME OF OUR BEST PILOTS.
OUR REPORTS INDICATE HIS STARFIGHTER IS VASTLY SUPERIOR TO ANYTHING WE HAVE IN SERVICE.
THERE IS A GREATER DANGER, I'M AFRAID--
--WITH EVERY VICTORY HE IS BECOMING AN INSTRUMENT OF PROPAGANDA. VANE IS A HERO OF THE CONFEDERACY.
HE MUST BE STOPPED. I'M SENDING YOU THE COMPLETE DOSSIER ON VANE.
I'VE ALREADY MEMORIZED IT, MASTER WINDU. I'M READY TO GO AFTER HIM IMMEDIATELY.
THAT MAY BE DIFFICULT. WE'VE SEARCHED THE SURROUNDING SYSTEMS BUT HAVEN'T BEEN ABLE TO LOCATE HIS BASE. IT MUST BE WELL CONCEALED.
DRAW VANE OUT OF HIDING, YOU MUST.
WE ANTICIPATE HIS NEXT ATTACK WILL BE IN THE HEXUS SYSTEM. GO THERE AND REINFORCE ADMIRAL ALDANNA'S BLOCKADE.
ARTOO, PREP MY FIGHTER FOR TAKEOFF.
AHSOKA, YOU AND ADMIRAL YULAREN GET THE FLEET READY AND FOLLOW ME AS SOON AS YOU CAN.
MAY THE FORCE BE WITH YOU, MASTER.

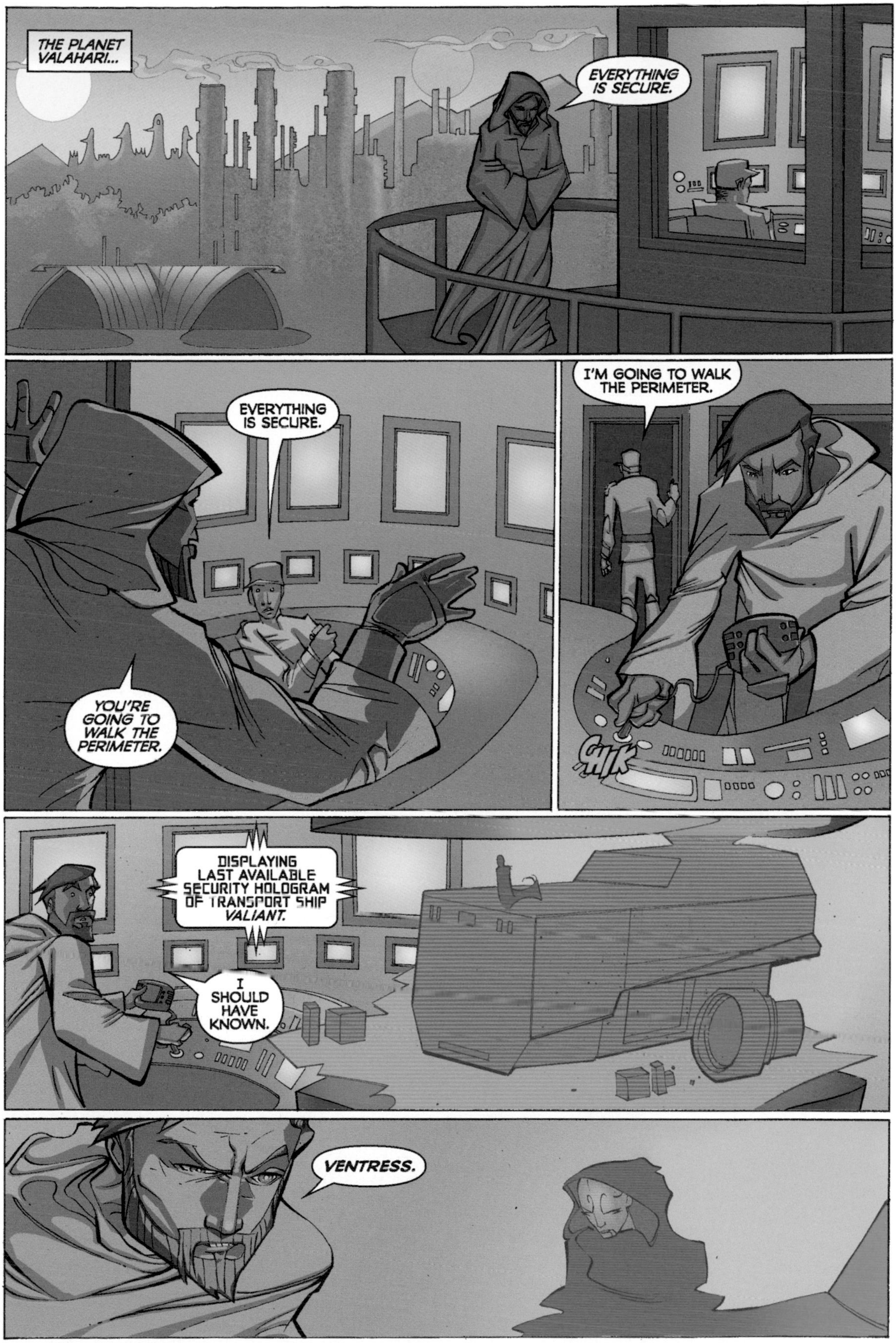
THE PLANET VALAHARI...
EVERYTHING IS SECURE.
EVERYTHING IS SECURE.
YOU'RE GOING TO WALK THE PERIMETER.
I'M GOING TO WALK THE PERIMETER.
CHIK
DISPLAYING LAST AVAILABLE SECURITY HOLOGRAM OF TRANSPORT SHIP VALIANT.
I SHOULD HAVE KNOWN.
VENTRESS.

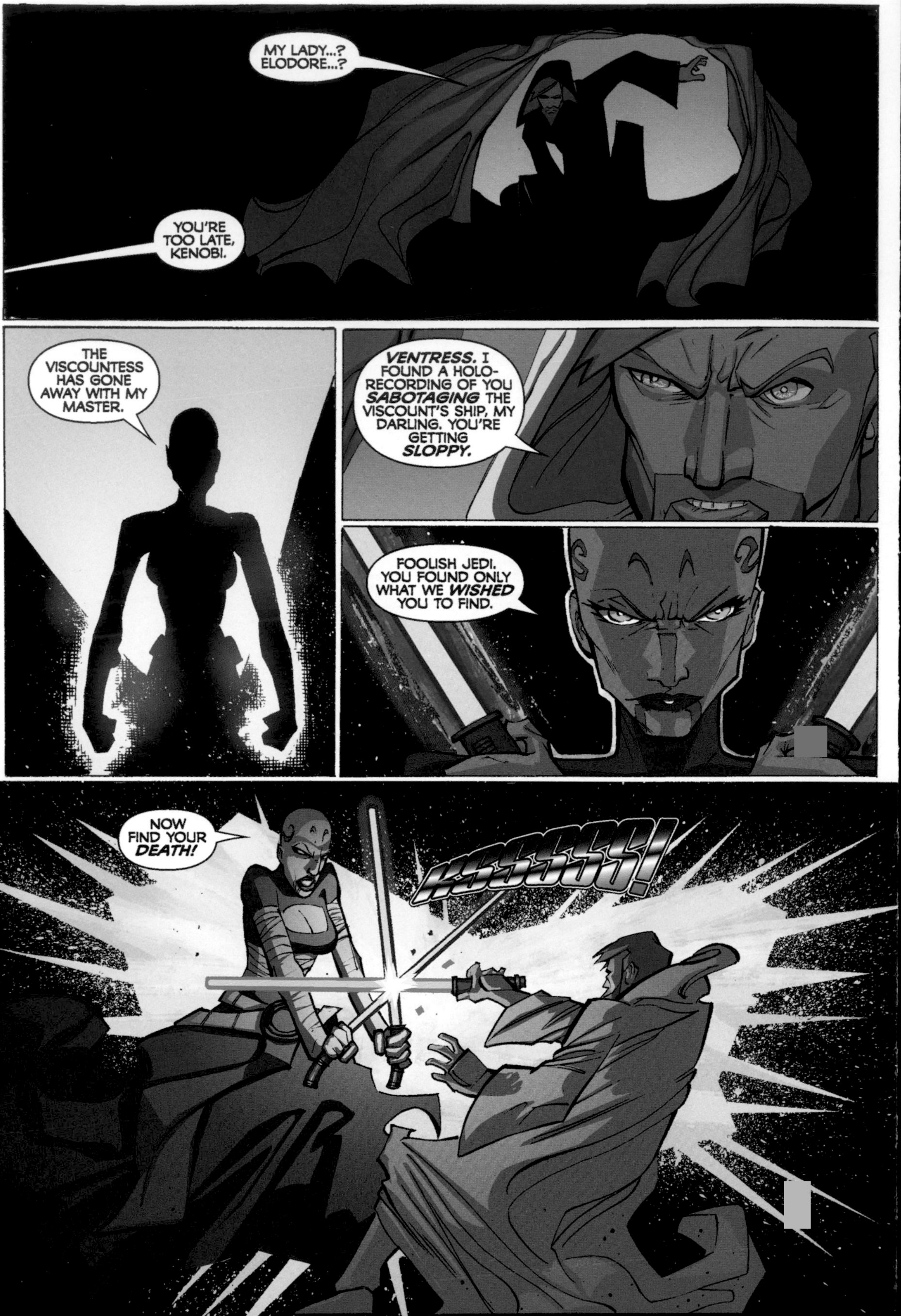
MY LADY...? ELODORE...?
YOU'RE TOO LATE, KENOBI.
THE VISCOUNTESS HAS GONE AWAY WITH MY MASTER.
VENTRESS. I FOUND A HOLO-RECORDING OF YOU *SABOTAGING* THE VISCOUNT'S SHIP, MY DARLING. YOU'RE GETTING *SLOPPY.*
FOOLISH JEDI. YOU FOUND ONLY WHAT WE *WISHED* YOU TO FIND.
NOW FIND YOUR *DEATH!*
KSSSSS!

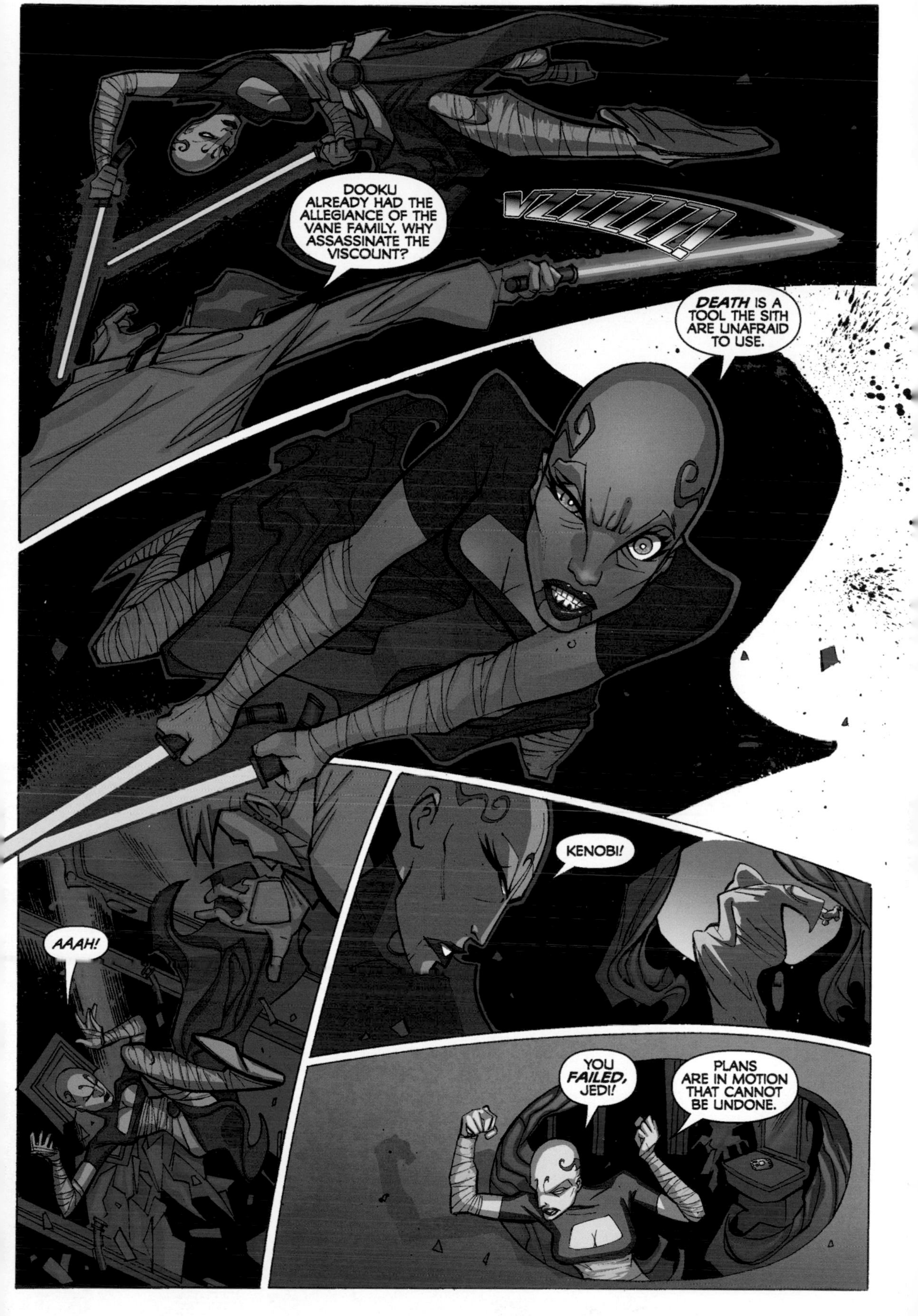
DOOKU ALREADY HAD THE ALLEGIANCE OF THE VANE FAMILY. WHY ASSASSINATE THE VISCOUNT?
VZZZZZZM!
DEATH IS A TOOL THE SITH ARE UNAFRAID TO USE.
AAAH!
KENOBI!
YOU FAILED, JEDI!
PLANS ARE IN MOTION THAT CANNOT BE UNDONE.

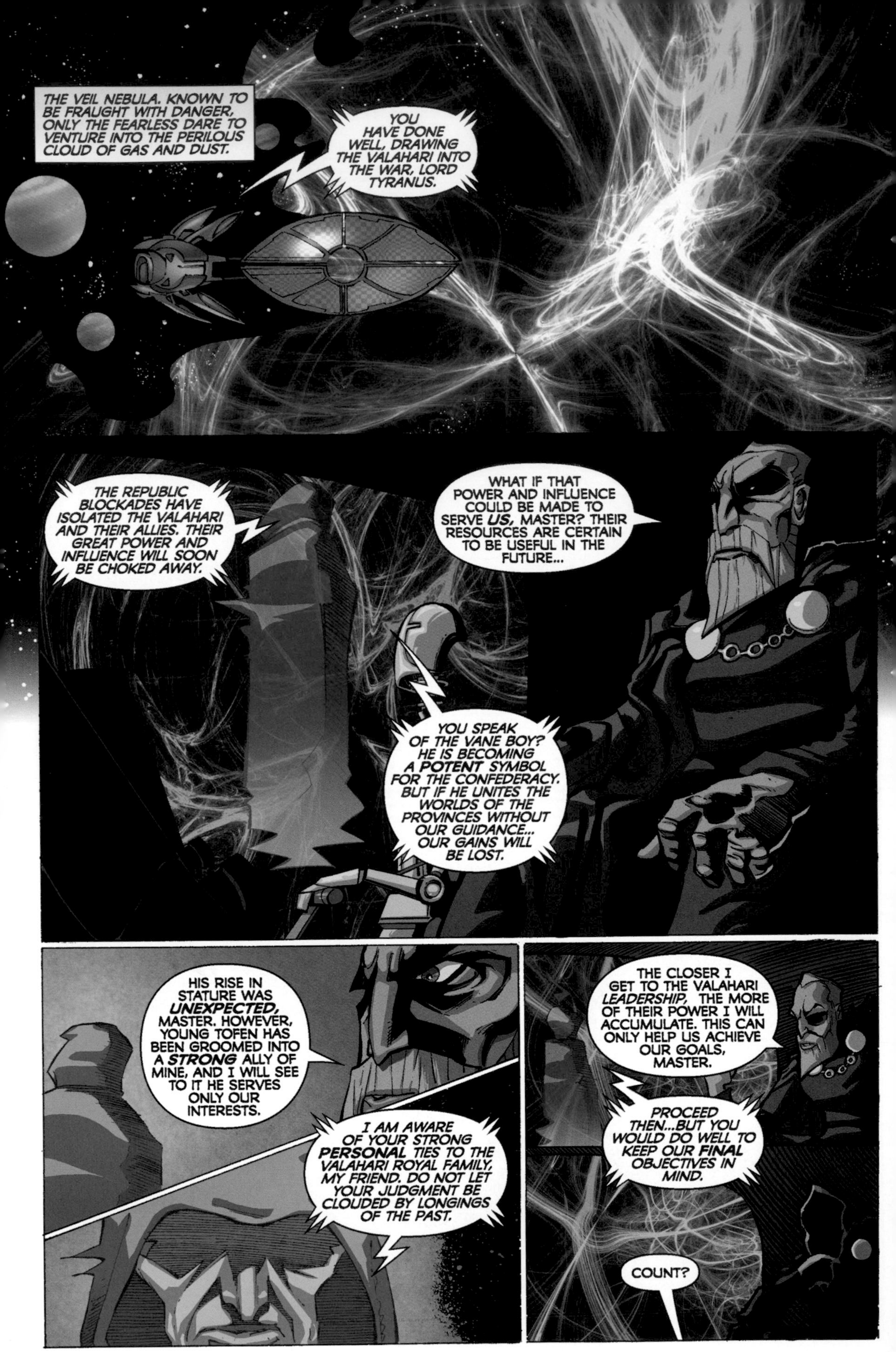
THE VEIL NEBULA. KNOWN TO BE FRAUGHT WITH DANGER, ONLY THE FEARLESS DARE TO VENTURE INTO THE PERILOUS CLOUD OF GAS AND DUST.
YOU HAVE DONE WELL, DRAWING THE VALAHARI INTO THE WAR, LORD TYRANUS.
THE REPUBLIC BLOCKADES HAVE ISOLATED THE VALAHARI AND THEIR ALLIES. THEIR GREAT POWER AND INFLUENCE WILL SOON BE CHOKED AWAY.
WHAT IF THAT POWER AND INFLUENCE COULD BE MADE TO SERVE US, MASTER? THEIR RESOURCES ARE CERTAIN TO BE USEFUL IN THE FUTURE...
YOU SPEAK OF THE VANE BOY? HE IS BECOMING A POTENT SYMBOL FOR THE CONFEDERACY. BUT IF HE UNITES THE WORLDS OF THE PROVINCES WITHOUT OUR GUIDANCE... OUR GAINS WILL BE LOST.
HIS RISE IN STATURE WAS UNEXPECTED, MASTER. HOWEVER, YOUNG TOFEN HAS BEEN GROOMED INTO A STRONG ALLY OF MINE, AND I WILL SEE TO IT HE SERVES ONLY OUR INTERESTS.
I AM AWARE OF YOUR STRONG PERSONAL TIES TO THE VALAHARI ROYAL FAMILY, MY FRIEND. DO NOT LET YOUR JUDGMENT BE CLOUDED BY LONGINGS OF THE PAST.
THE CLOSER I GET TO THE VALAHARI LEADERSHIP, THE MORE OF THEIR POWER I WILL ACCUMULATE. THIS CAN ONLY HELP US ACHIEVE OUR GOALS, MASTER.
PROCEED THEN...BUT YOU WOULD DO WELL TO KEEP OUR FINAL OBJECTIVES IN MIND.
COUNT?

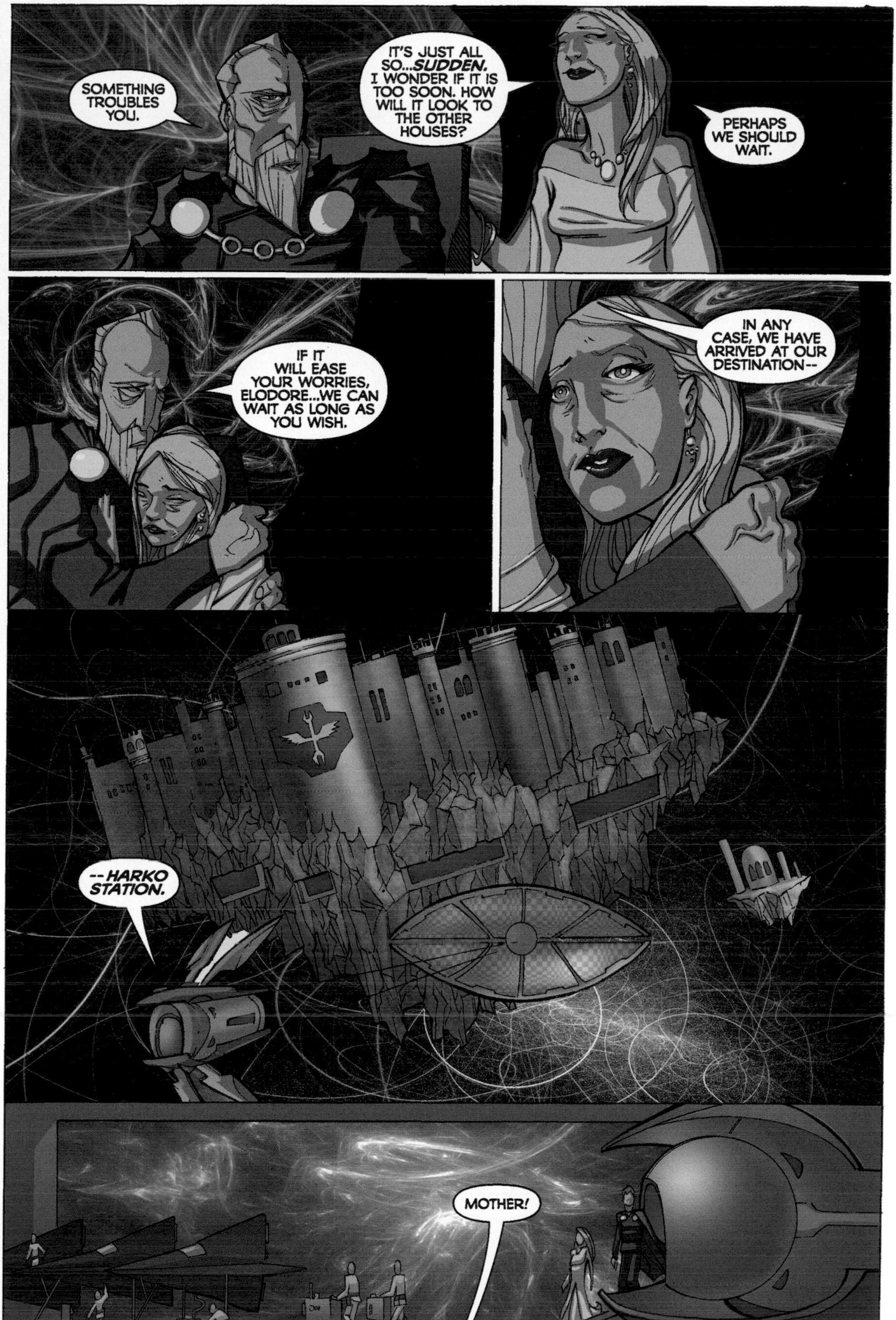
SOMETHING TROUBLES YOU.
IT'S JUST ALL SO...SUDDEN. I WONDER IF IT IS TOO SOON. HOW WILL IT LOOK TO THE OTHER HOUSES?
PERHAPS WE SHOULD WAIT.
IF IT WILL EASE YOUR WORRIES, ELODORE...WE CAN WAIT AS LONG AS YOU WISH.
IN ANY CASE, WE HAVE ARRIVED AT OUR DESTINATION--
--HARKO STATION.
MOTHER!

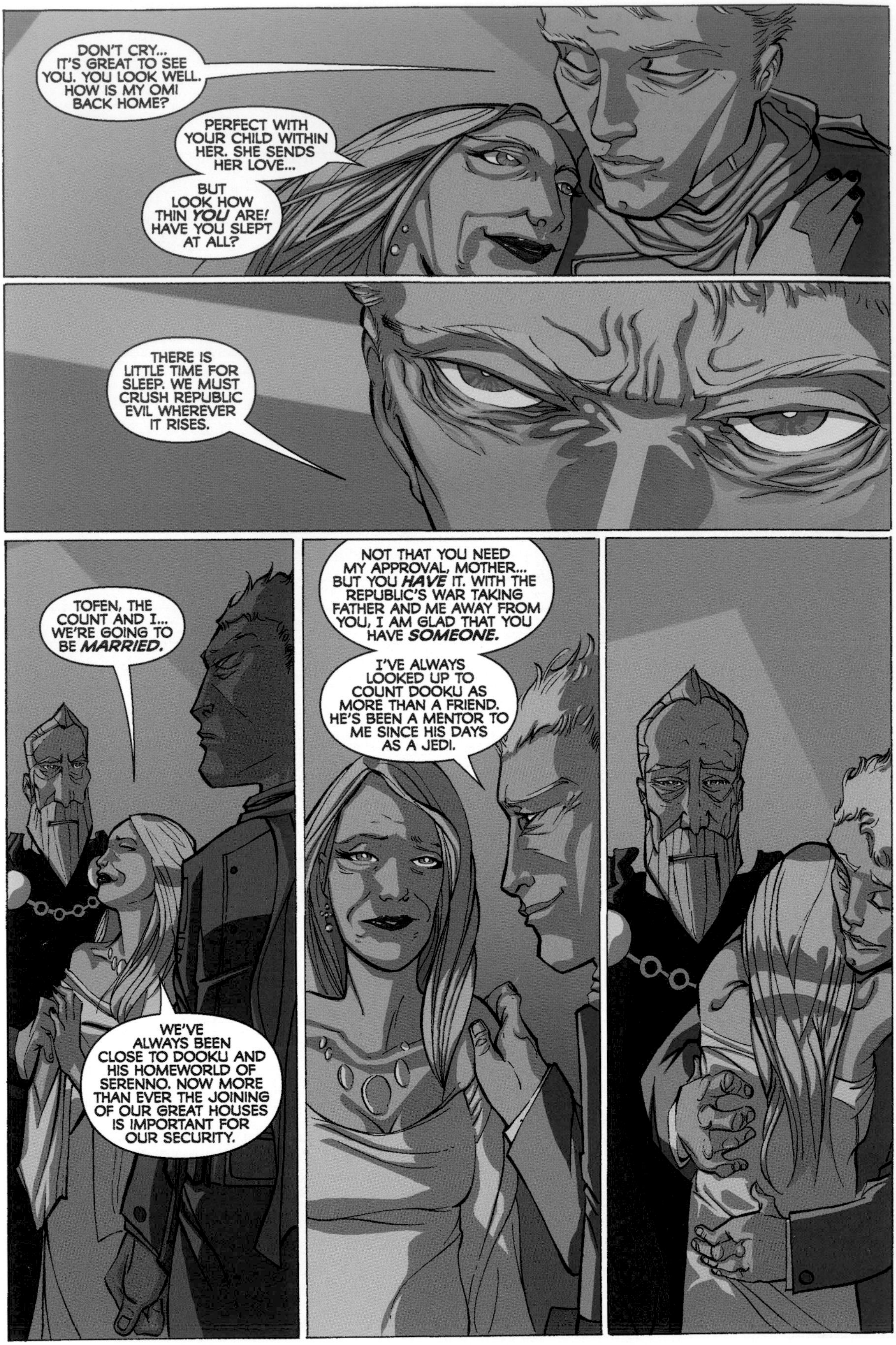
DON'T CRY... IT'S GREAT TO SEE YOU. YOU LOOK WELL. HOW IS MY OMI BACK HOME?
PERFECT WITH YOUR CHILD WITHIN HER. SHE SENDS HER LOVE...
BUT LOOK HOW THIN *YOU* ARE! HAVE YOU SLEPT AT ALL?
THERE IS LITTLE TIME FOR SLEEP. WE MUST CRUSH REPUBLIC EVIL WHEREVER IT RISES.
TOFEN, THE COUNT AND I... WE'RE GOING TO BE ***MARRIED.***
WE'VE ALWAYS BEEN CLOSE TO DOOKU AND HIS HOMEWORLD OF SERENNO. NOW MORE THAN EVER THE JOINING OF OUR GREAT HOUSES IS IMPORTANT FOR OUR SECURITY.
NOT THAT YOU NEED MY APPROVAL, MOTHER... BUT YOU ***HAVE*** IT. WITH THE REPUBLIC'S WAR TAKING FATHER AND ME AWAY FROM YOU, I AM GLAD THAT YOU HAVE ***SOMEONE.***
I'VE ALWAYS LOOKED UP TO COUNT DOOKU AS MORE THAN A FRIEND. HE'S BEEN A MENTOR TO ME SINCE HIS DAYS AS A JEDI.

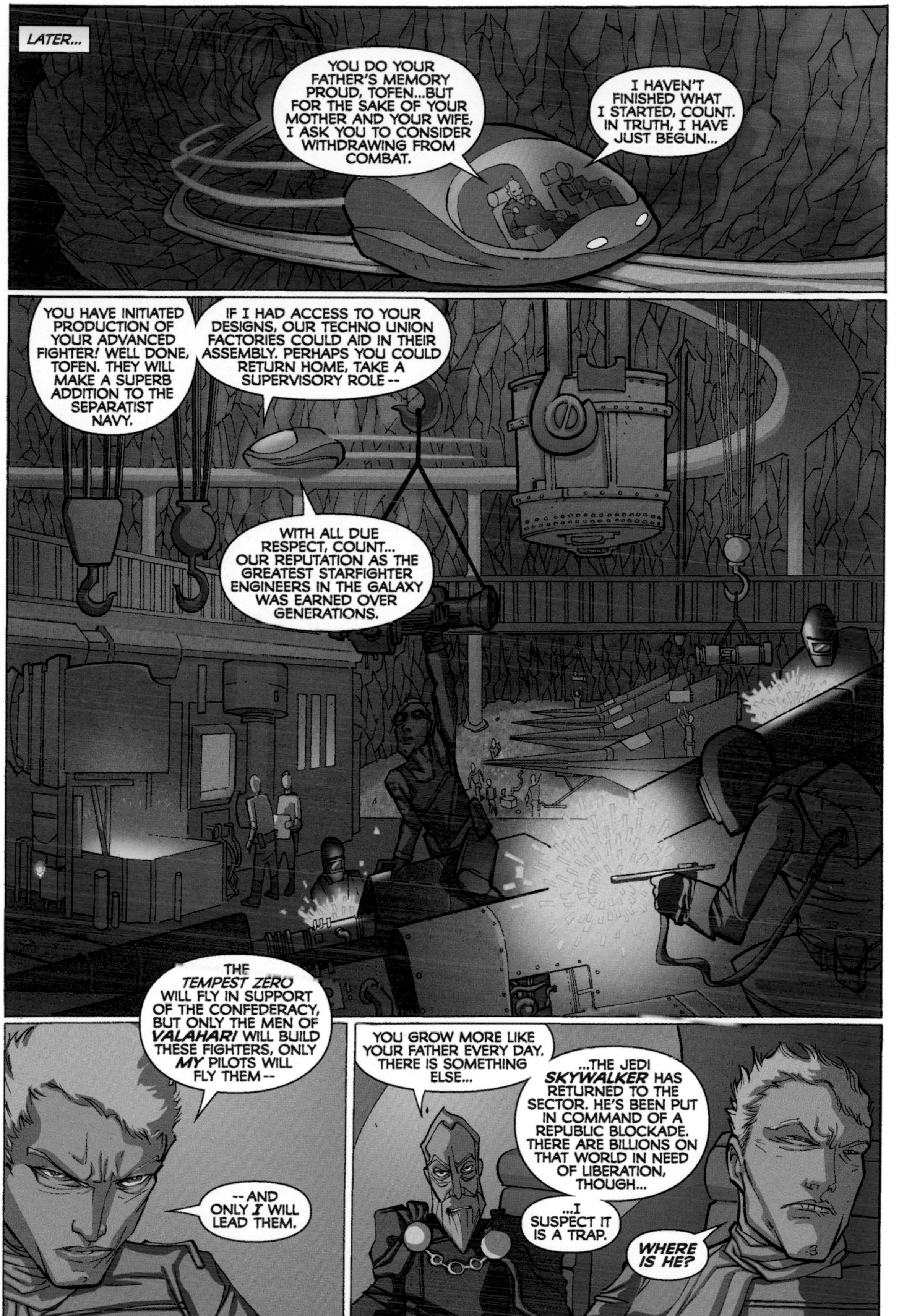
LATER...
YOU DO YOUR FATHER'S MEMORY PROUD, TOFEN...BUT FOR THE SAKE OF YOUR MOTHER AND YOUR WIFE, I ASK YOU TO CONSIDER WITHDRAWING FROM COMBAT.
I HAVEN'T FINISHED WHAT I STARTED, COUNT. IN TRUTH, I HAVE JUST BEGUN...
YOU HAVE INITIATED PRODUCTION OF YOUR ADVANCED FIGHTER! WELL DONE, TOFEN. THEY WILL MAKE A SUPERB ADDITION TO THE SEPARATIST NAVY.
IF I HAD ACCESS TO YOUR DESIGNS, OUR TECHNO UNION FACTORIES COULD AID IN THEIR ASSEMBLY. PERHAPS YOU COULD RETURN HOME, TAKE A SUPERVISORY ROLE --
WITH ALL DUE RESPECT, COUNT... OUR REPUTATION AS THE GREATEST STARFIGHTER ENGINEERS IN THE GALAXY WAS EARNED OVER GENERATIONS.
THE *TEMPEST ZERO* WILL FLY IN SUPPORT OF THE CONFEDERACY, BUT ONLY THE MEN OF *VALAHARI* WILL BUILD THESE FIGHTERS, ONLY *MY* PILOTS WILL FLY THEM --
-- AND ONLY *I* WILL LEAD THEM.
YOU GROW MORE LIKE YOUR FATHER EVERY DAY. THERE IS SOMETHING ELSE...
...THE JEDI *SKYWALKER* HAS RETURNED TO THE SECTOR. HE'S BEEN PUT IN COMMAND OF A REPUBLIC BLOCKADE. THERE ARE BILLIONS ON THAT WORLD IN NEED OF LIBERATION, THOUGH...
...I SUSPECT IT IS A TRAP.
WHERE IS HE?

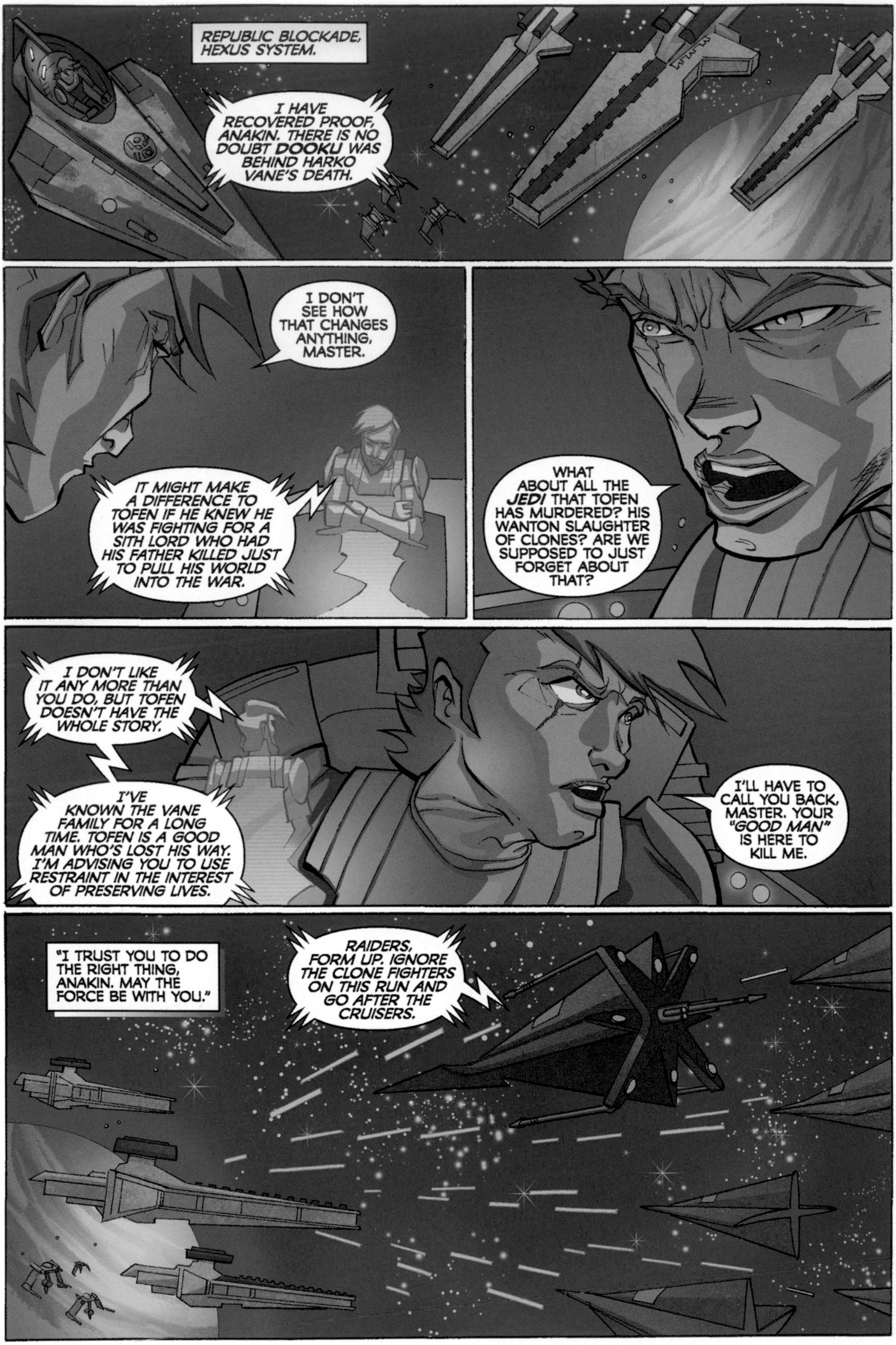
REPUBLIC BLOCKADE, HEXUS SYSTEM.
I HAVE RECOVERED PROOF, ANAKIN. THERE IS NO DOUBT DOOKU WAS BEHIND HARKO VANE'S DEATH.
I DON'T SEE HOW THAT CHANGES ANYTHING, MASTER.
IT MIGHT MAKE A DIFFERENCE TO TOFEN IF HE KNEW HE WAS FIGHTING FOR A SITH LORD WHO HAD HIS FATHER KILLED JUST TO PULL HIS WORLD INTO THE WAR.
WHAT ABOUT ALL THE JEDI THAT TOFEN HAS MURDERED? HIS WANTON SLAUGHTER OF CLONES? ARE WE SUPPOSED TO JUST FORGET ABOUT THAT?
I DON'T LIKE IT ANY MORE THAN YOU DO, BUT TOFEN DOESN'T HAVE THE WHOLE STORY.
I'VE KNOWN THE VANE FAMILY FOR A LONG TIME. TOFEN IS A GOOD MAN WHO'S LOST HIS WAY. I'M ADVISING YOU TO USE RESTRAINT IN THE INTEREST OF PRESERVING LIVES.
I'LL HAVE TO CALL YOU BACK, MASTER. YOUR "GOOD MAN" IS HERE TO KILL ME.
"I TRUST YOU TO DO THE RIGHT THING, ANAKIN. MAY THE FORCE BE WITH YOU."
RAIDERS, FORM UP. IGNORE THE CLONE FIGHTERS ON THIS RUN AND GO AFTER THE CRUISERS.

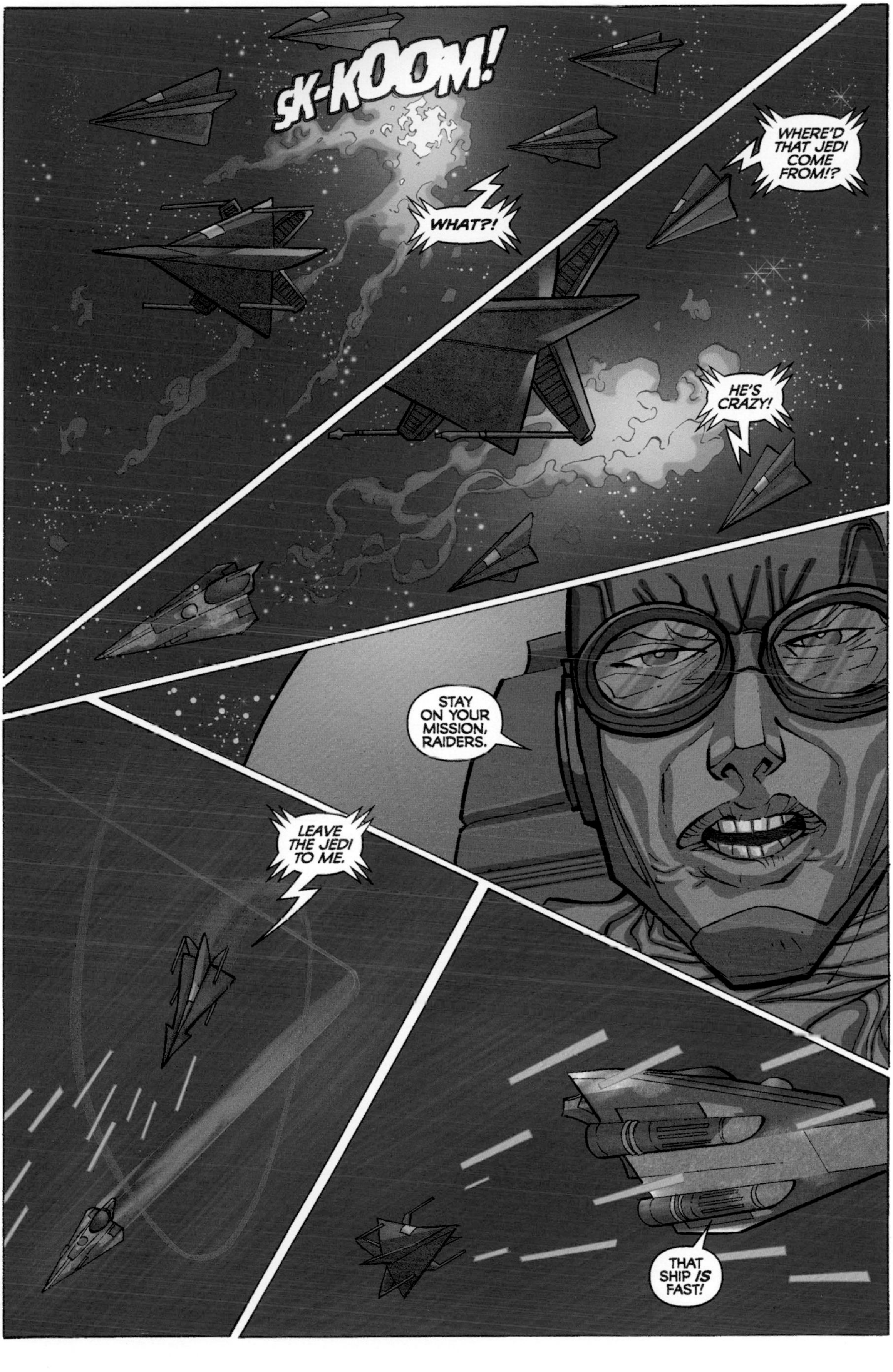
SK-KOOM!
WHAT?!
WHERE'D THAT JEDI COME FROM!?
HE'S CRAZY!
STAY ON YOUR MISSION, RAIDERS.
LEAVE THE JEDI TO ME.
THAT SHIP IS FAST!

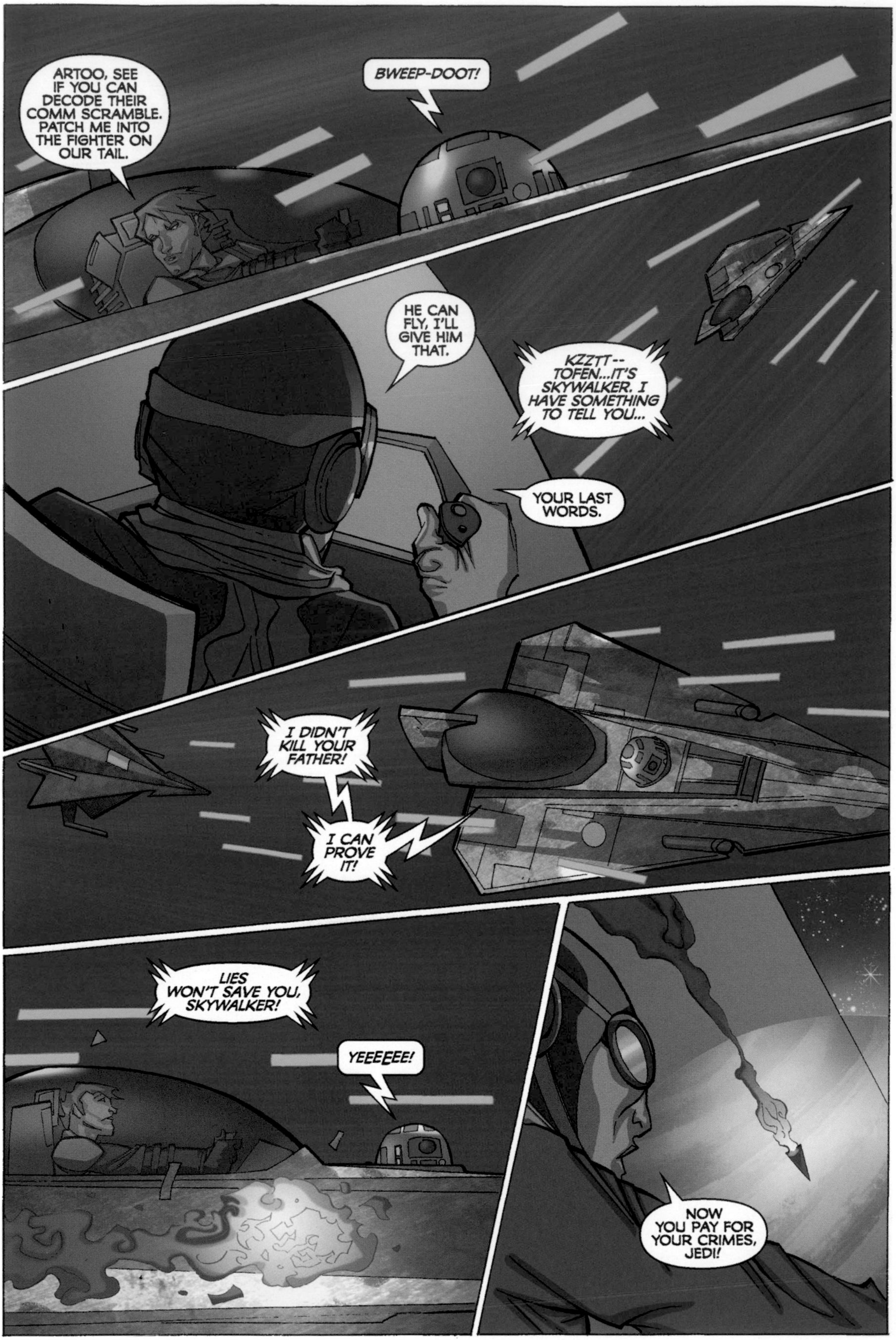
ARTOO, SEE IF YOU CAN DECODE THEIR COMM SCRAMBLE. PATCH ME INTO THE FIGHTER ON OUR TAIL.
BWEEP-DOOT!
HE CAN FLY, I'LL GIVE HIM THAT.
KZZTT-- TOFEN...IT'S SKYWALKER. I HAVE SOMETHING TO TELL YOU...
YOUR LAST WORDS.
I DIDN'T KILL YOUR FATHER!
I CAN PROVE IT!
LIES WON'T SAVE YOU, SKYWALKER!
YEEEEEE!
NOW YOU PAY FOR YOUR CRIMES, JEDI!

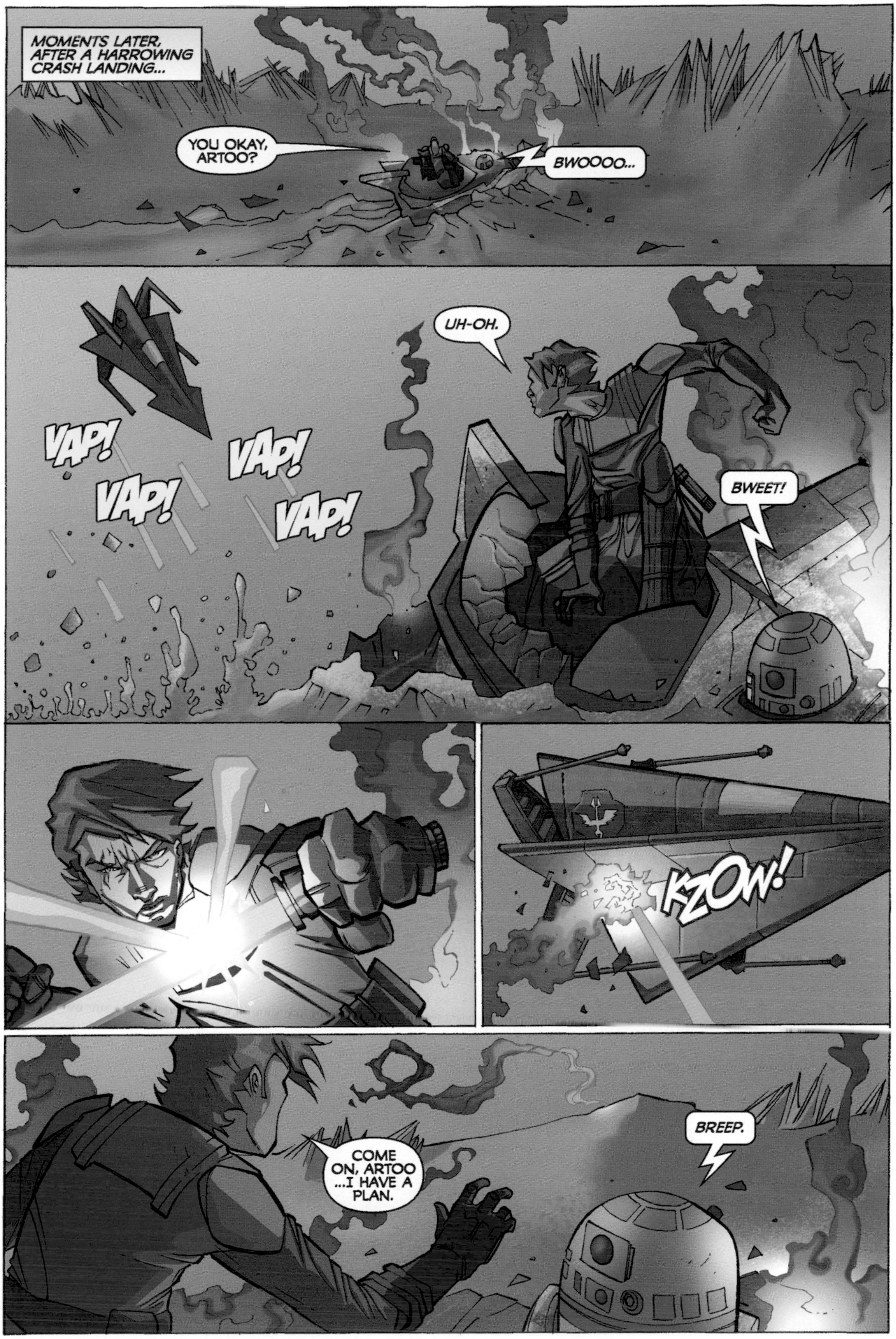
MOMENTS LATER, AFTER A HARROWING CRASH LANDING...
YOU OKAY, ARTOO?
BWOOOO...
UH-OH.
VAP!
VAP!
VAP!
VAP!
BWEET!
KZOW!
COME ON, ARTOO ...I HAVE A PLAN.
BREEP.

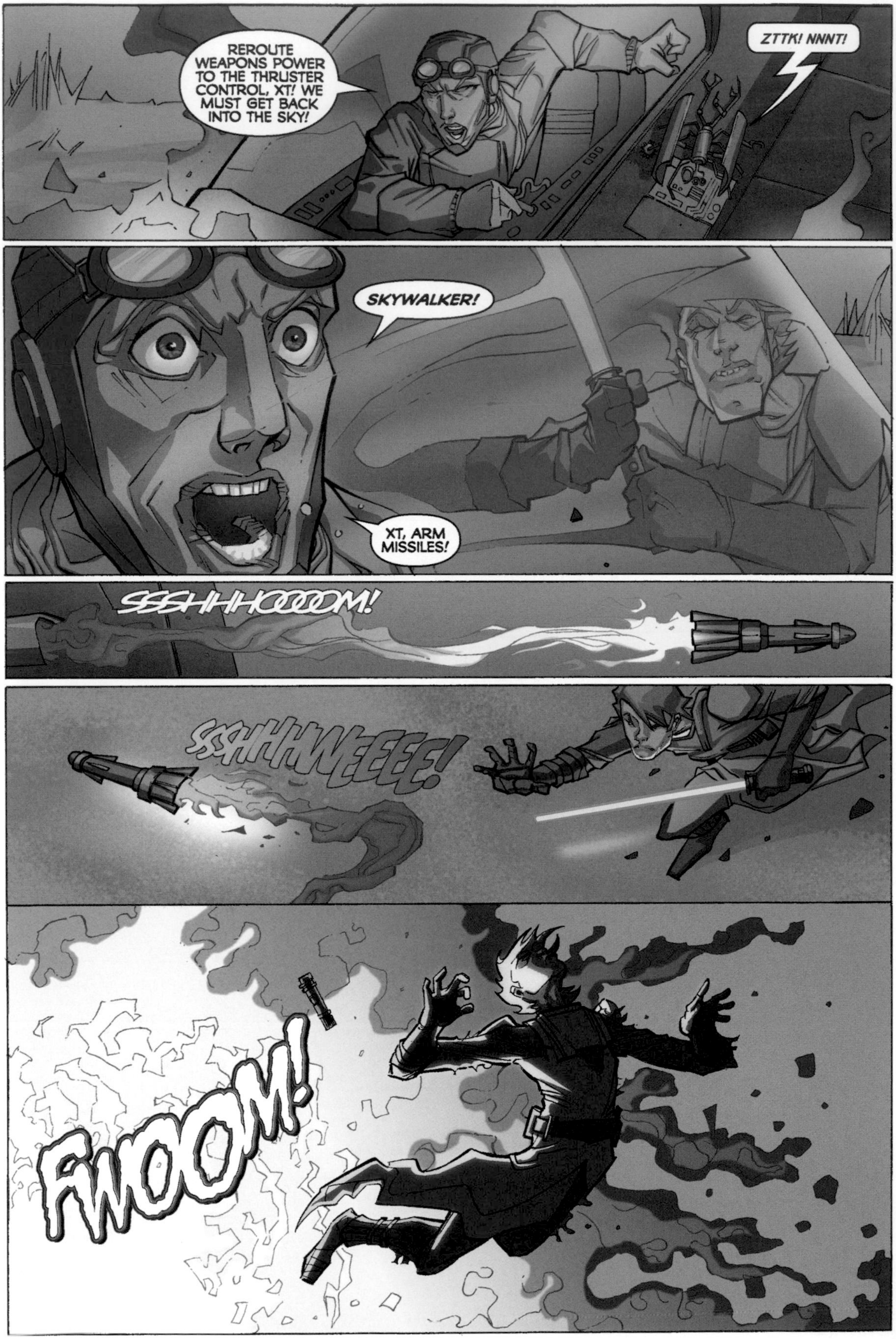
REROUTE WEAPONS POWER TO THE THRUSTER CONTROL, XT! WE MUST GET BACK INTO THE SKY!
ZTTK! NNNT!
SKYWALKER!
XT, ARM MISSILES!
SSSHHHOOOOM!
SSSHHHWEEEE!
FWOOM!

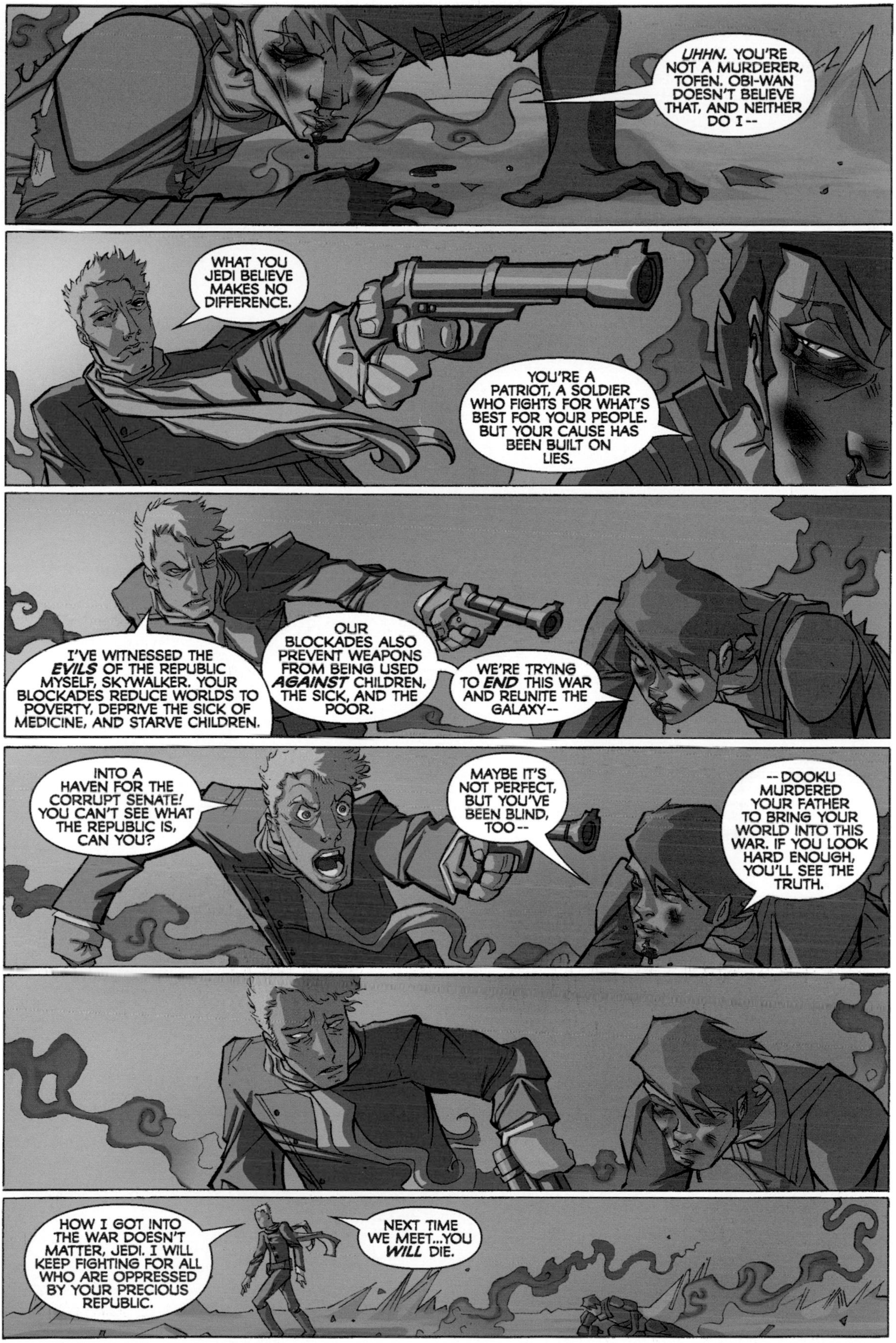
UHHN. YOU'RE NOT A MURDERER, TOFEN. OBI-WAN DOESN'T BELIEVE THAT, AND NEITHER DO I--
WHAT YOU JEDI BELIEVE MAKES NO DIFFERENCE.
YOU'RE A PATRIOT, A SOLDIER WHO FIGHTS FOR WHAT'S BEST FOR YOUR PEOPLE. BUT YOUR CAUSE HAS BEEN BUILT ON LIES.
I'VE WITNESSED THE EVILS OF THE REPUBLIC MYSELF, SKYWALKER. YOUR BLOCKADES REDUCE WORLDS TO POVERTY, DEPRIVE THE SICK OF MEDICINE, AND STARVE CHILDREN.
OUR BLOCKADES ALSO PREVENT WEAPONS FROM BEING USED AGAINST CHILDREN, THE SICK, AND THE POOR.
WE'RE TRYING TO END THIS WAR AND REUNITE THE GALAXY--
INTO A HAVEN FOR THE CORRUPT SENATE! YOU CAN'T SEE WHAT THE REPUBLIC IS, CAN YOU?
MAYBE IT'S NOT PERFECT, BUT YOU'VE BEEN BLIND, TOO--
--DOOKU MURDERED YOUR FATHER TO BRING YOUR WORLD INTO THIS WAR. IF YOU LOOK HARD ENOUGH, YOU'LL SEE THE TRUTH.
HOW I GOT INTO THE WAR DOESN'T MATTER, JEDI. I WILL KEEP FIGHTING FOR ALL WHO ARE OPPRESSED BY YOUR PRECIOUS REPUBLIC.
NEXT TIME WE MEET...YOU WILL DIE.

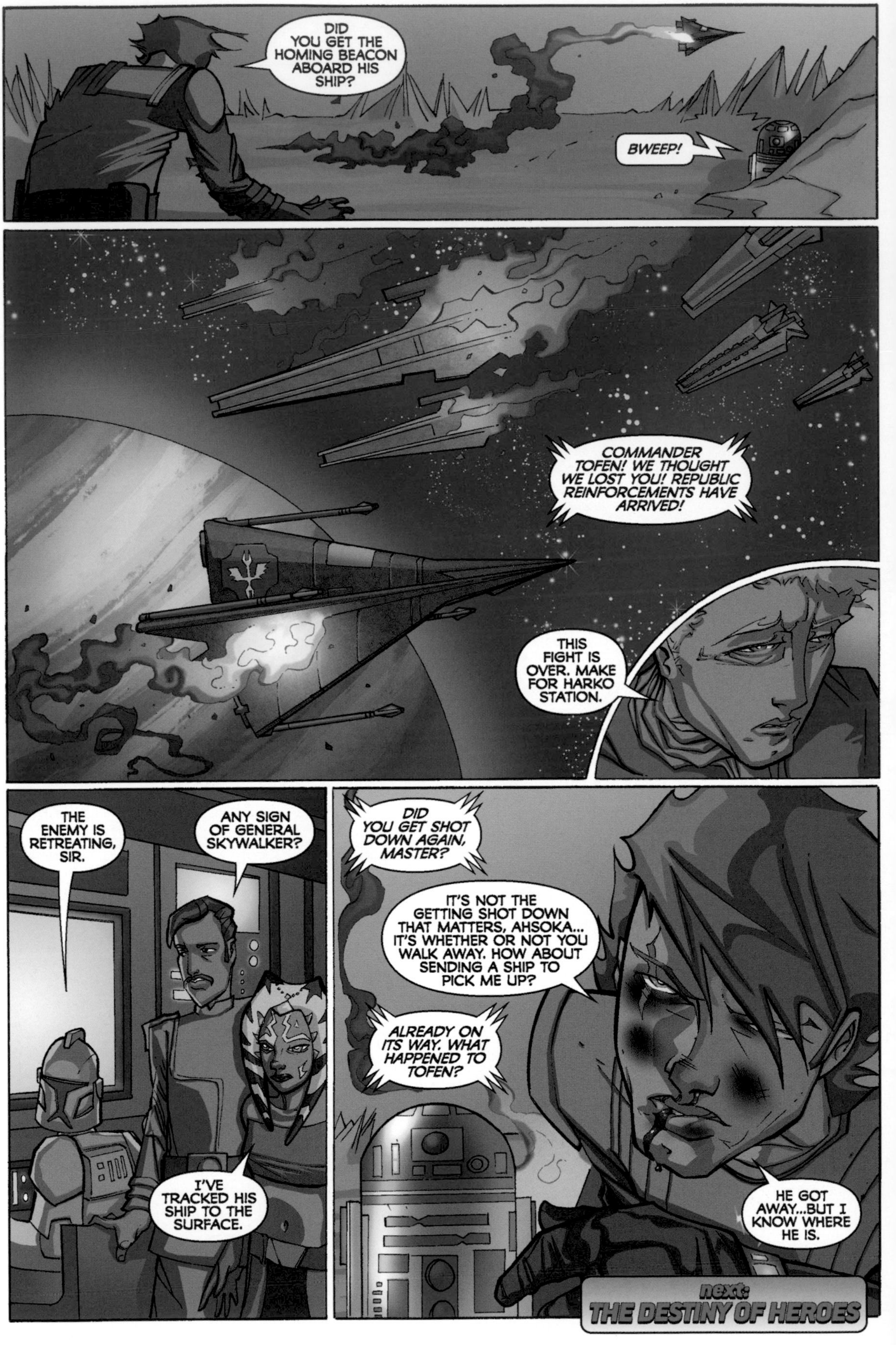
DID YOU GET THE HOMING BEACON ABOARD HIS SHIP?
BWEEP!
COMMANDER TOFEN! WE THOUGHT WE LOST YOU! REPUBLIC REINFORCEMENTS HAVE ARRIVED!
THIS FIGHT IS OVER. MAKE FOR HARKO STATION.
THE ENEMY IS RETREATING, SIR.
ANY SIGN OF GENERAL SKYWALKER?
I'VE TRACKED HIS SHIP TO THE SURFACE.
DID YOU GET SHOT DOWN AGAIN, MASTER?
IT'S NOT THE GETTING SHOT DOWN THAT MATTERS, AHSOKA... IT'S WHETHER OR NOT YOU WALK AWAY. HOW ABOUT SENDING A SHIP TO PICK ME UP?
ALREADY ON ITS WAY. WHAT HAPPENED TO TOFEN?
HE GOT AWAY...BUT I KNOW WHERE HE IS.
next:
THE DESTINY OF HEROES